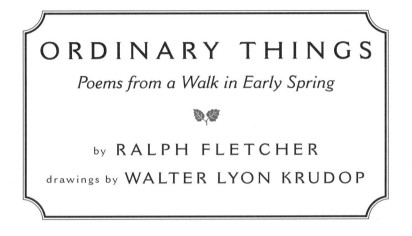

# ORDINARY THINGS

*Poems from a Walk in Early Spring*

by RALPH FLETCHER

drawings by WALTER LYON KRUDOP

ATHENEUM BOOKS FOR YOUNG READERS

Atheneum Books for Young Readers
An imprint of Simon & Schuster Children's Publishing Division
1230 Avenue of the Americas
New York, New York 10020

Book design by Michael Nelson

The text of this book is set in Cantoria.
The illustrations are rendered in pencil.

First Edition
Printed in the United States of America
10 9 8 7 6 5 4

Library of Congress Cataloging-in-Publication Data
Fletcher, Ralph J.
Ordinary things : poems from a walk in early spring / by
Ralph Fletcher ; drawings by Walter Lyon Krudop.
p.   cm.
Summary: A collection of poems recall the sights and feelings
experienced on a springtime walk—from home, through the woods,
and back again.
ISBN 0-689-81035-0
1. Nature—Juvenile poetry. 2. Spring—Juvenile poetry. 3. Children's poetry,
American. [1. American poetry. 2. Nature—Poetry. 3. Spring—Poetry.]
I. Krudop, Walter, ill. II. Title.
PS3556.L523073   1997
811'.54—dc20
96-3393

*For Adam Curtis*
*—R. F.*

*For Mark*
*—W. L. K.*

# CONTENTS

## WALKING

## INTO THE WOODS

## LOOPING BACK

# WALKING

Time to leave my desk
and leave the house,
pulling the door behind.

I walk the way I write
starting out all creaky,
sort of stumbling along,
looking for a rhythm.

Each footstep is like a word
as it meets the blank page
followed by a pause
before the next one:
step, step, word . . .

## wind

the calendar says it's early spring
but the wind pretends not to know

it reaches with bone-cold fingers
inside my coat to rattle my ribs

it swoops down into my mouth
stuns my tongue, steals my voice

it whispers secrets past my ear a
blur of words too fast too low

## stone walls

Centuries ago wiry farmers
cleared granite from the throat
of their land to build these walls.

Stone divided farm from farm
so one man's livestock wouldn't
savage another man's crops.

Now the crumbling walls remain
content to stop small trees from
getting loose and running amuck.

## clothesline

There's an orange towel and
two white t-shirts pinned
at the waist all trying to
dry themselves in the
breeze.

Filled with air the two t-shirts
puff up with sudden bodies
real and muscular which
vanish when the wind
dies.

The wind lifts the towel until
it lies horizontal as if trying
to screw up the nerve
to let go and
fly

**running water**

dripping off rooftops
liquified diamonds
lit by clean light

babbling snow-melt
bringing the gossip
spilling off mountains

young
      laughing
            running
                  water

## maple syrup buckets

At the edge of Mr. Wells's woods
I count eighteen rusty buckets
hanging from maple trees.

In these parts it's a known fact
that Mr. Wells has never smiled
in fact hardly speaks at all

though he once explained to me
why it takes forty gallons of sap
to make a single gallon of syrup

which made me wonder if maybe
he requires forty hours of silence
to make a single hour of talk.

He keeps bees, too: succulent honey.
Strange that such a sour man should
produce all that sweetness.

## telephone pole

Once it was a rooted tree
with nests and songbirds
that sighed and shooshed
in the wash of the wind.

Its roots have all been cut.
Birds still visit but only
voices and voltage
sing through its wires.

A swallow once built a nest
but a man pulled it down
and carefully spliced
a nest of cables.

litter

What geniuses left this trash?
I walk past abandoned tires,
beer bottles, one red sneaker,

not to mention the other stuff.
Trees never clean up their
leavesleavesleavesleaves. . . .

And all these rocks! Blame
the glacier for scattering
this litter of stone.

## stream

No place better than a stream
to think out a tough decision
or just sit back and dream.

No one built the winding paths
that stream waters follow
except water and rock and land.

Stream decisions take time
and water is world famous
for stopping to change its mind.

## fossil

right behind that swamp
wedged in a piece of flat rock

I once found a fossilized clam
a million-year-old mollusk

which tells me all this dry land
once lay beneath a great ocean

so I hold my breath as I walk
and think *all this underwater*

## soon

soon the clouds like dark dough
pressed against invisible glass

soon the rain to turn the grass
so green it will make you stare

soon the nests filled with chirps
raining down like confetti bits

soon you'll be able to walk at night
breathing sweet blossoms unseen

# INTO
# THE
# WOODS

No sidewalks around here so I
walk at the road's furthest edge

along with this floatsam and jetsam:
bolts, gravel, crushed cigarette packs.

Every atom of me came from the earth
which originally was part of the sun.

I am starstuff, every part of me,
but my life feels much too tame.

It's high time I head into the woods,
the last wild place around.

# myriad

I've learned a new word,
(*myriad:* many, countless)
and fly it like a new kite
while I hike these woods

     myriad tiny twigs
     myriad swollen buds
     myriad insects stirring
     beneath the muddy earth

**baby fern**

the shoot
slowly uncurls
like a slender
green finger
pointing up
at the sun

## waiting for music

Tight buds loosen
and tiny fists bring
gifts: new leaves
pea green and shy.

The leaves will become
uncountable chimes
played and replayed
by the rustling wind.

Listen to the earth's first
music, lovely and common
like the beating of rain
or the beating of hearts.

### architecture

This is one school subject
I can never keep straight:

the architecture of columns
Ionic, Doric, and Corinthian.

Greek columns remind me
of the mighty trunks of trees.

The supple way they sway
in the teeth of the wind.

The majestic support they give
to temples of leaves and light.

## birches

Snow tries to keep clean
but the dirt always shows.
White is the trickiest color

which may help to explain
why you hardly ever get
white in a box of crayons.

Only birches make it work,
lines drawn bold and white
down the sky's blue canvas.

## birds' nests

You see birds' nests
like unpicked fruit
in branches bare
of any leaves.

When I was small
Grandma cut my hair
and tossed the clumps
onto our lawn.

"Birds will use it
to line their nests
and keep the eggs
safe and warm."

An amazing thing:
my ordinary hair
woven into a bird's
wild tapestry.

## undecided

The sun sprays
summery light
but the wind speaks
with winter's tongue.

The pond reflects
so much cloudy blue
I can't quite decide
whether it's the sky

using the pond
as a mirror
or the pond wearing
bracelets of sky.

### arrowhead

Always keep my eyes alert
for the telltale tip of an
arrowhead.

You can find them around here
sharp enough to draw
blood.

Strange that I know almost
nothing about the people
who first walked this land.

> *their myths and songs*
> *the sound of their words*

I'm looking for an arrowhead.
I want to hold one in my hand.
I want to touch the tip of history.

## rock dreams

rock
protruding from the earth
remembers the thrusting glacier
that one day left it
behind

rock
reflected in the water
shimmers against the brilliant sky
like a rock's wavery dream
of dance

## circles

That leaf in the pond
slowly spinning a
round.

That hawk circling
in a circumference of
death.

Those six dry leaves
playing ring around
a rosie.

The stacked firewood
a collection of rings
within rings.

At that large boulder
I'll start to loop
back home.

# LOOPING

# BACK

*Something tugs as I walk along:*
*the familiar pull of gravity.*

*That large bird with spread wings*
*riding invisible wind currents*

*pulls me toward the sky.*
*Not to mention the road itself.*

*In Ireland they say the road*
*flows with or against you*

*like the current of a river*
*(or the flow of written words).*

*And now I feel this new tug*
*pulling me toward home.*

## snakeskin

I stop at an ordinary rock
at the edge of a stream.
Three times I have found

skins from a garter snake,
strips of cloudy cellophane
that let light shine through.

Why do snakes pick this spot
this rock among all others
to rub off their old skins?

I decide to stop right here
and unwrap my sandwich,
rub my back against this rock

which feels amazingly solid,
as good a place as any
to make a new start.

## leaves

I find a streaked yellow leaf
among the sea of browns
and save it for Mrs. Lyons.

Twelve years she taught school
in Guam, a tropical paradise.
Each autumn a package arrived,

very light but Mrs. Lyons knew
exactly what she'd find inside:
a bunch of bright fall leaves

from a friend back in Vermont.
There in Guam she'd open the box
and spill them all over the house,

lovely leaves, a whole rug of them,
so many hues from so far away,
and then she would start to cry.

## mailboxes

When I step from the forest
onto the hard black asphalt
my eyes start playing tricks.

That fire hydrant turns into
a toddler dressed to the gills
in a snug winter snowsuit.

See those mailboxes over there?
To me they look like old people
dancing slowly cheek-to-cheek.

### beetle

Who knows the story
behind this VW Bug
white and well-rusted,

utterly abandoned
to a meadow of weeds
and wild blackberries?

Who knows how it got
turned on its back
tires pointed up

like an unlucky beetle
who never learned to
turn back over?

## douglas firs

The douglas firs sit alone and uncut
in a peaceful corner of the meadow.

Planted in five long straight lines
meant for blinking lights and tinsel

they escaped by growing too tall
in an unsung Christmas miracle.

I walk through the uniform rows
rub shoulders with tall survivors

picture them here in happy solitude
winter branches bright with ice

decked with fireflies in the summer
and silver milkweed spores come fall.

## water magic

Hawaii has rainbows
almost every day.

The Arctic boasts
the *aurora borealis*.

The magic around here
is rooted in water.

A farmer once cut
a forked wooden bough

and showed me how
to divine for water.

"Walk!" he said
and my feet obeyed

'til my hands felt the bough
pull down hard. "Water!"

I tell my hands: *Impossible*
but they know what they felt.

## horses

Okay, I'll admit it: I don't love them.
Have never wanted to own one,

feel hot horse breath on my cheek.
Never dreamed of riding bareback

through the foamy surf of a beach
or anywhere else for that matter.

Don't thrill to their liquid walk,
can't tell a canter from a trot.

But the way that raw horse smell
strikes my nostrils from far off,

the way they raise furred heads
to gaze at me so nonchalantly

makes me glad to be walking
through a stretch of their world.

### daffodils

they put on a little show
simply by being so yellow
their stems darkly green
against the faded brown barn

## apple trees

Leafless and almost ugly,
with limbs freshly pruned
they look like old gnomes
half-hidden in the mist.

I seem to have caught them
in a strange ballet, motionless,
this tree frozen while trying
a comical pirouette,

that one just about to leap,
its gnarled limbs flung back.
They will resume dancing
as soon as I pass by.

### railroad tracks

I got built ninety years back by
sweating stinking swearing men.

For decades every kind of train
screeched on my back. No more.

Winters here can be pretty bleak
but wildflowers always come back.

Empty nests have that forlorn look
'til the songbirds return in May.

The swamp is quiet but soon frogs
will take up their monotonous chant.

My back remains unbroken but only
ghost locomotives rattle these rails.

*walking*

*I walk to wash the dead air*
*from the branches of my lungs*

*I walk to let some actual oxygen*
*carbonate the blood in my veins*

*I walk to let my toes and soles*
*know the yielding feel of earth*

*I walk to rinse all these words*
*from my head*